JOURNEY TO THE CENTER OF THE EARTH

Adapted by

Joeming Dunn

Illustrated by

Rod Espinosa

Based upon the works of

Jules Verne

magic
Wagon

visit us at
www.abdopublishing.com

Published by Magic Wagon, a division of the ABDO Group, 8000 West 78th Street, Edina, Minnesota 55439. Copyright © 2010 by Abdo Consulting Group, Inc. International copyrights reserved in all countries. All rights reserved. No part of this book may be reproduced in any form without written permission from the publisher.

Graphic Planet™ is a trademark and logo of Magic Wagon.

Printed in the United States.

 Manufactured with paper containing at least 10% post-consumer waste

Based upon the works of Jules Verne
Adapted by Joeming Dunn
Illustrated by Rod Espinosa
Colored and lettered by Rod Espinosa
Edited by Stephanie Hedlund and Rochelle Baltzer
Interior layout and design by Antarctic Press
Cover art by Rod Espinosa
Cover design by Neil Klinepier

Library of Congress Cataloging-in-Publication Data

Dunn, Joeming W.
  Journey to the center of the earth / adapted by Joeming Dunn ; illustrated by Rod Espinosa ; based upon the works of Jules Verne.
      p. cm. -- (Graphic planet. Graphic horror)
  Summary: A graphic novel based on the Jules Verne classic, in which a group of people journey into the crater of a volcano to find the center of the earth.
  ISBN 978-1-60270-678-1 (alk. paper)
  1. Graphic novels. [1. Graphic novels. 2. Verne, Jules, 1828-1905. Voyage au centre de la terre--Adaptations. 3. Science fiction.] I. Espinosa, Rod, ill. II. Verne, Jules, 1828-1905. Voyage au centre de la terre. English. III. Title.
  PZ7.7.D86Jou 2010
  741.5'973--dc22
                                    2009008588

TABLE OF CONTENTS

Descend, bold traveler, into the crater of the jokul of Sneffels, which the shadow of Scartaris touches before the kalends of July, and you will attain the center of the earth; which I have done.

Arne Saknussemm

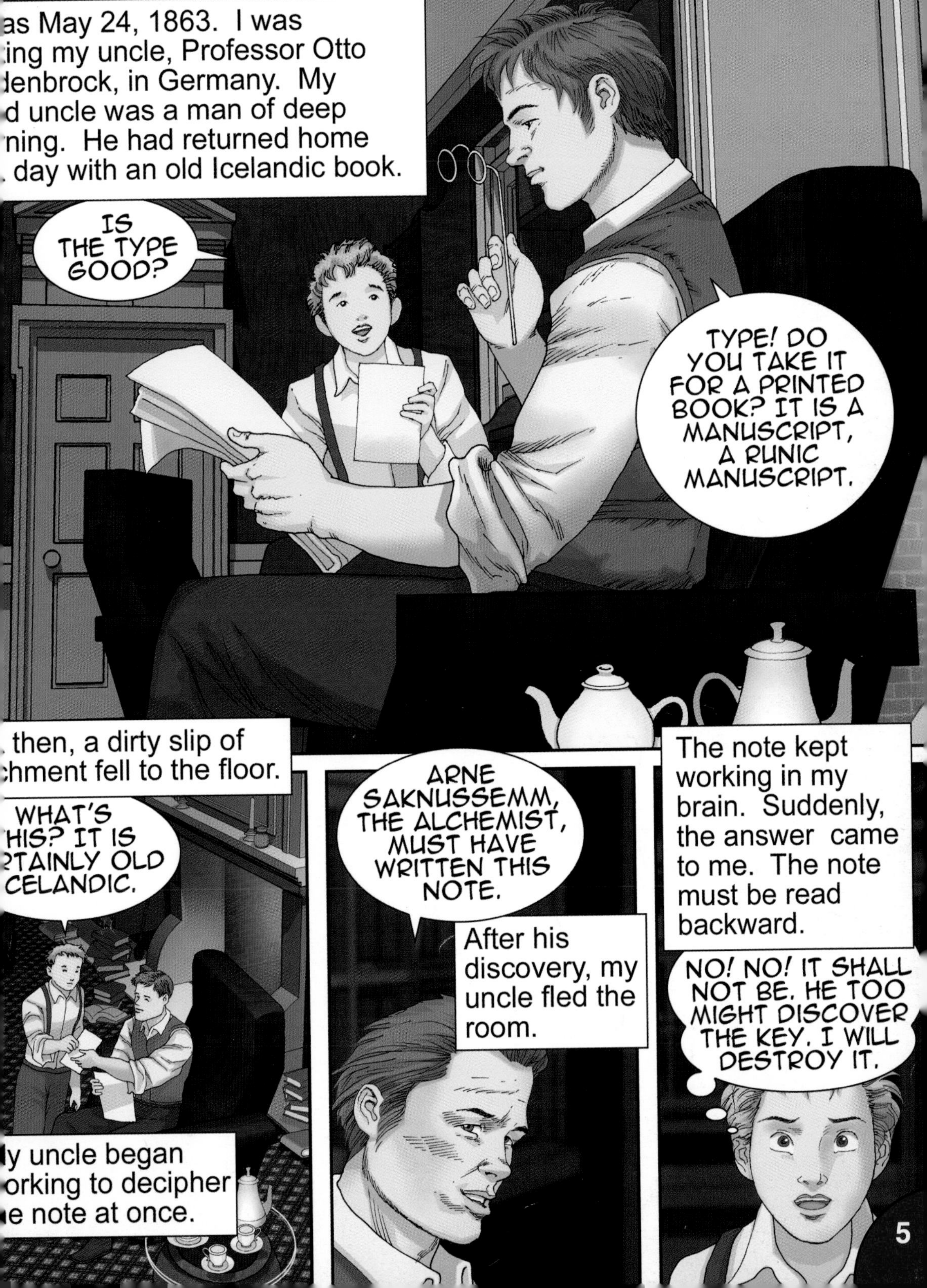
as May 24, 1863. I was
ing my uncle, Professor Otto
lenbrock, in Germany. My
d uncle was a man of deep
ning. He had returned home
. day with an old Icelandic book.
IS THE TYPE GOOD?
TYPE! DO YOU TAKE IT FOR A PRINTED BOOK? IT IS A MANUSCRIPT, A RUNIC MANUSCRIPT.
then, a dirty slip of
chment fell to the floor.
WHAT'S HIS? IT IS RTAINLY OLD CELANDIC.
ly uncle began
orking to decipher
e note at once.
ARNE SAKNUSSEMM, THE ALCHEMIST, MUST HAVE WRITTEN THIS NOTE.
After his discovery, my uncle fled the room.
The note kept working in my brain. Suddenly, the answer came to me. The note must be read backward.
NO! NO! IT SHALL NOT BE. HE TOO MIGHT DISCOVER THE KEY. I WILL DESTROY IT.

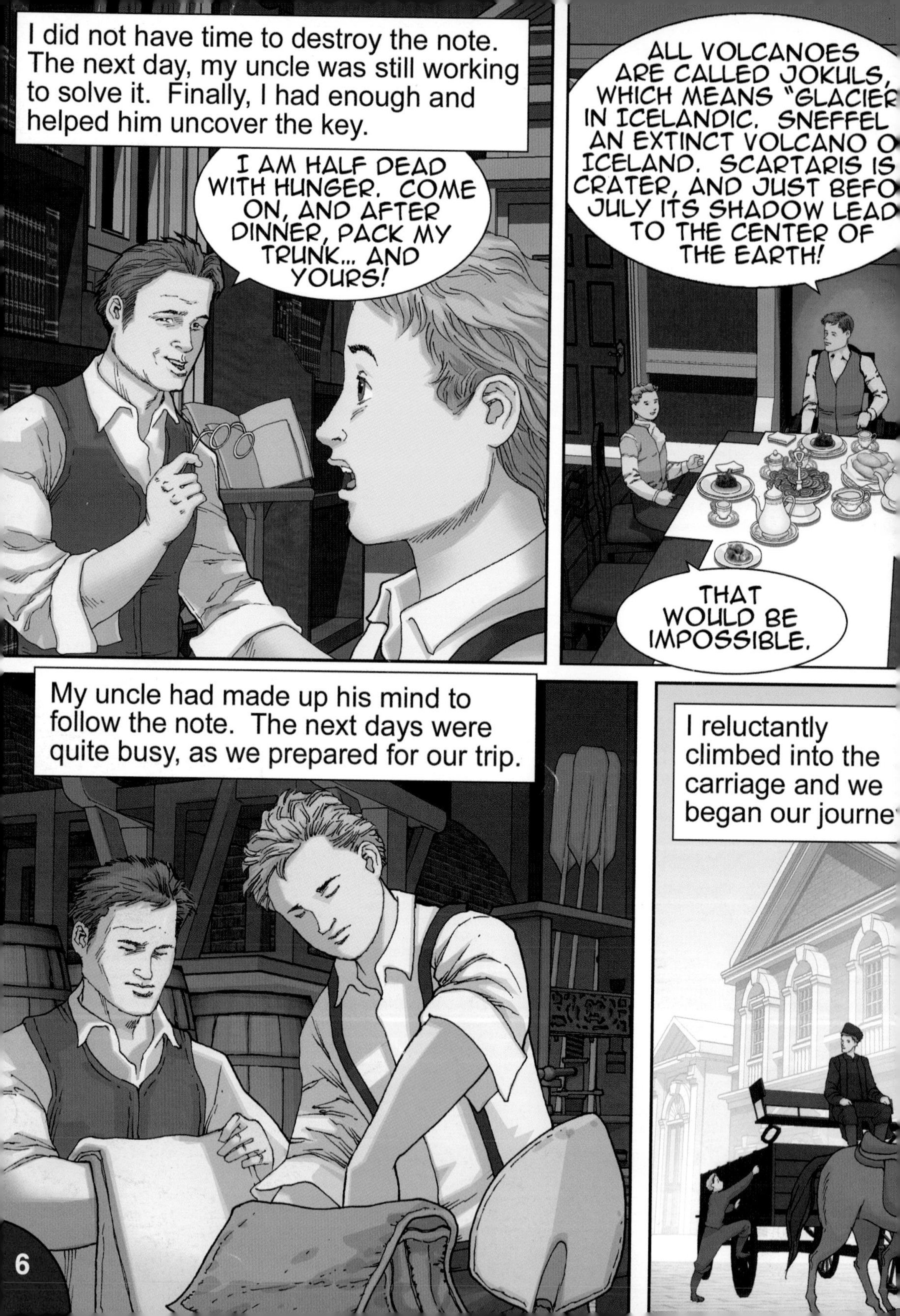
I did not have time to destroy the note. The next day, my uncle was still working to solve it. Finally, I had enough and helped him uncover the key.
I AM HALF DEAD WITH HUNGER. COME ON, AND AFTER DINNER, PACK MY TRUNK... AND YOURS!
ALL VOLCANOES ARE CALLED JOKULS, WHICH MEANS "GLACIER IN ICELANDIC. SNEFFEL AN EXTINCT VOLCANO O ICELAND. SCARTARIS IS CRATER, AND JUST BEFO JULY ITS SHADOW LEAD TO THE CENTER OF THE EARTH!
THAT WOULD BE IMPOSSIBLE.
My uncle had made up his mind to follow the note. The next days were quite busy, as we prepared for our trip.
I reluctantly climbed into the carriage and we began our journe

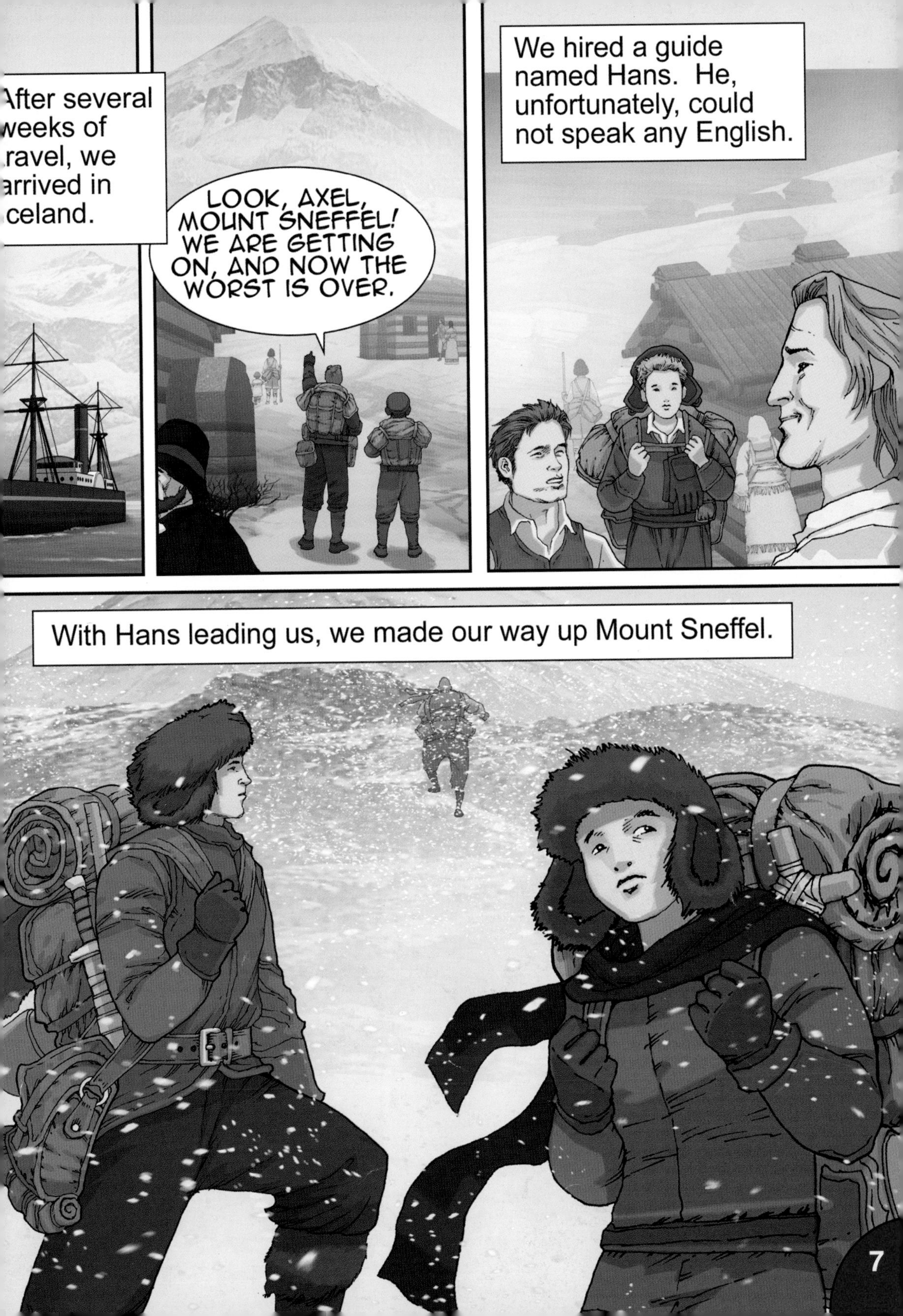
After several weeks of ravel, we arrived in celand.
LOOK, AXEL, MOUNT SNEFFEL! WE ARE GETTING ON, AND NOW THE WORST IS OVER.
We hired a guide named Hans. He, unfortunately, could not speak any English.
With Hans leading us, we made our way up Mount Sneffel.

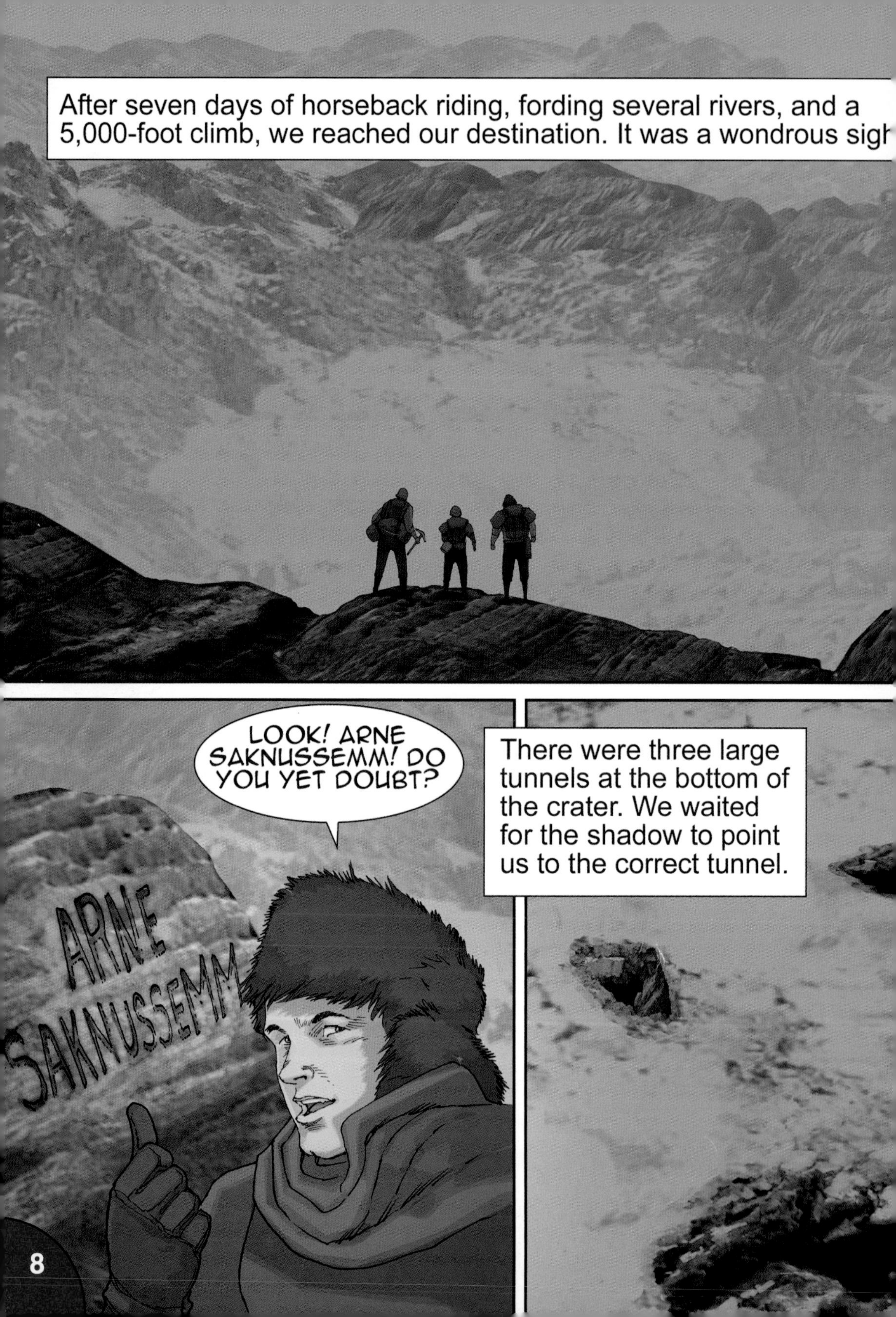
After seven days of horseback riding, fording several rivers, and a 5,000-foot climb, we reached our destination. It was a wondrous sigh
LOOK! ARNE SAKNUSSEMM! DO YOU YET DOUBT?
ARNE SAKNUSSEMM
There were three large tunnels at the bottom of the crater. We waited for the shadow to point us to the correct tunnel.

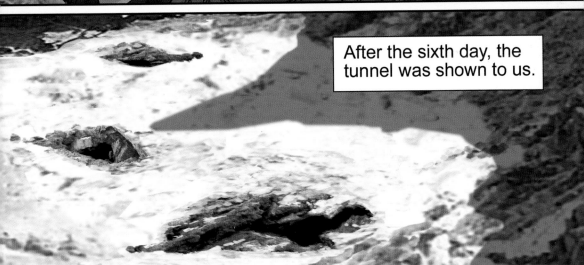

After the sixth day, the tunnel was shown to us.

My nerves made me shiver as we peered down the hole.

NOW FOR THE CENTER OF THE GLOBE!

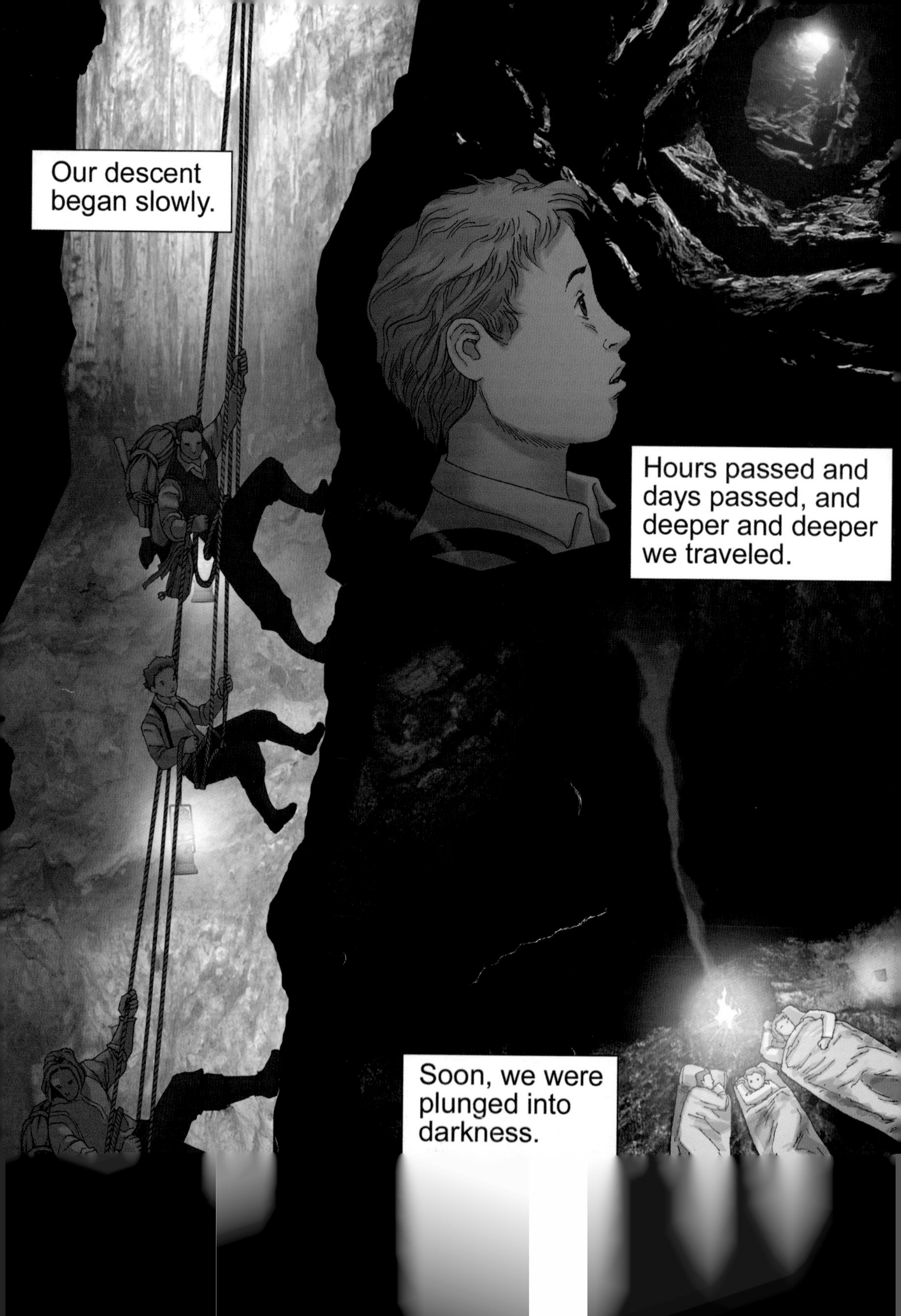
Our descent began slowly.
Hours passed and days passed, and deeper and deeper we traveled.
Soon, we were plunged into darkness.

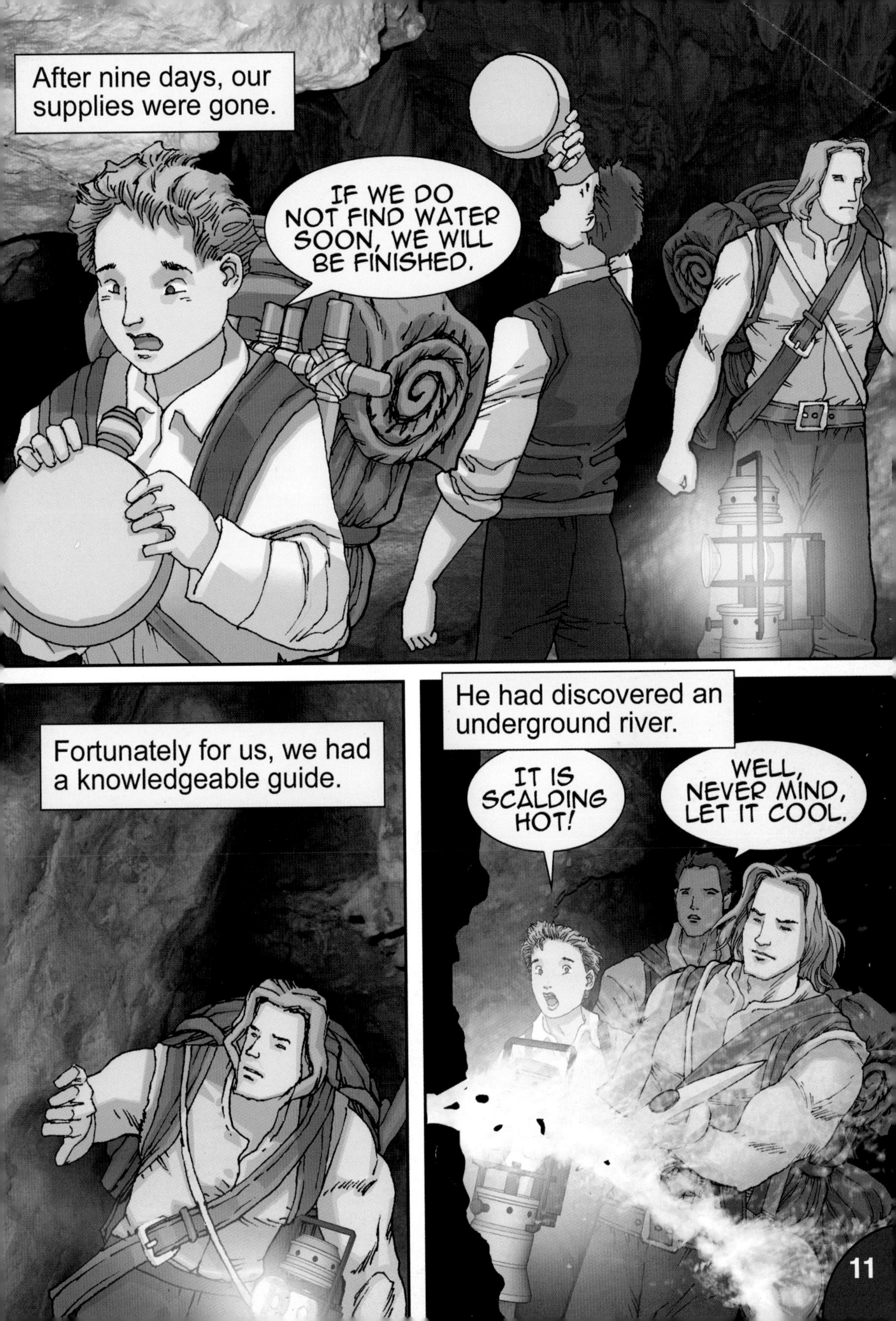
After nine days, our supplies were gone.
IF WE DO NOT FIND WATER SOON, WE WILL BE FINISHED.
Fortunately for us, we had a knowledgeable guide.
He had discovered an underground river.
IT IS SCALDING HOT!
WELL, NEVER MIND, LET IT COOL.

We rested that night and began again the next day. We continued for several days.

IF YOUR CALCULATIONS ARE CORRECT, WE HAVE TRAVELED 4,800 MILES DOWN INTO THE EARTH IN 20 DAYS.

SO YOU SAY.

IF WE HAVE GONE SO DEEP, THE TEMPERATURE SHOULD BE UNBEARABLE. YET IT IS ONLY 82°F.

SO THE CENTER OF THE EARTH MAY NOT BE AS HOT AS WE SUSPECTED.

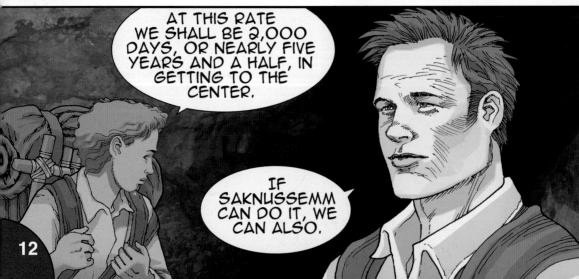

AT THIS RATE WE SHALL BE 2,000 DAYS, OR NEARLY FIVE YEARS AND A HALF, IN GETTING TO THE CENTER.

IF SAKNUSSEMM CAN DO IT, WE CAN ALSO.

continued to be filled with danger. Thanks to Hans, we crossed many a spot which we should never have cleared alone.

On the seventh of August, I got separated from Hans and my uncle.

HELLO... HELLO... HANS! UNCLE!

I thought I was now destined to die, buried alive deep within the Earth.

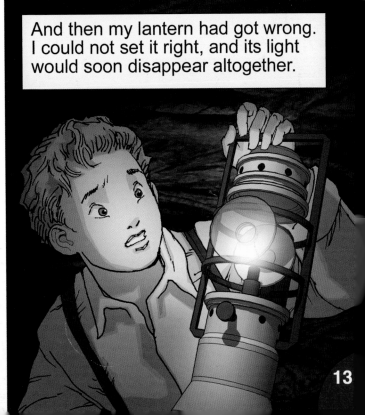

And then my lantern had got wrong. I could not set it right, and its light would soon disappear altogether.

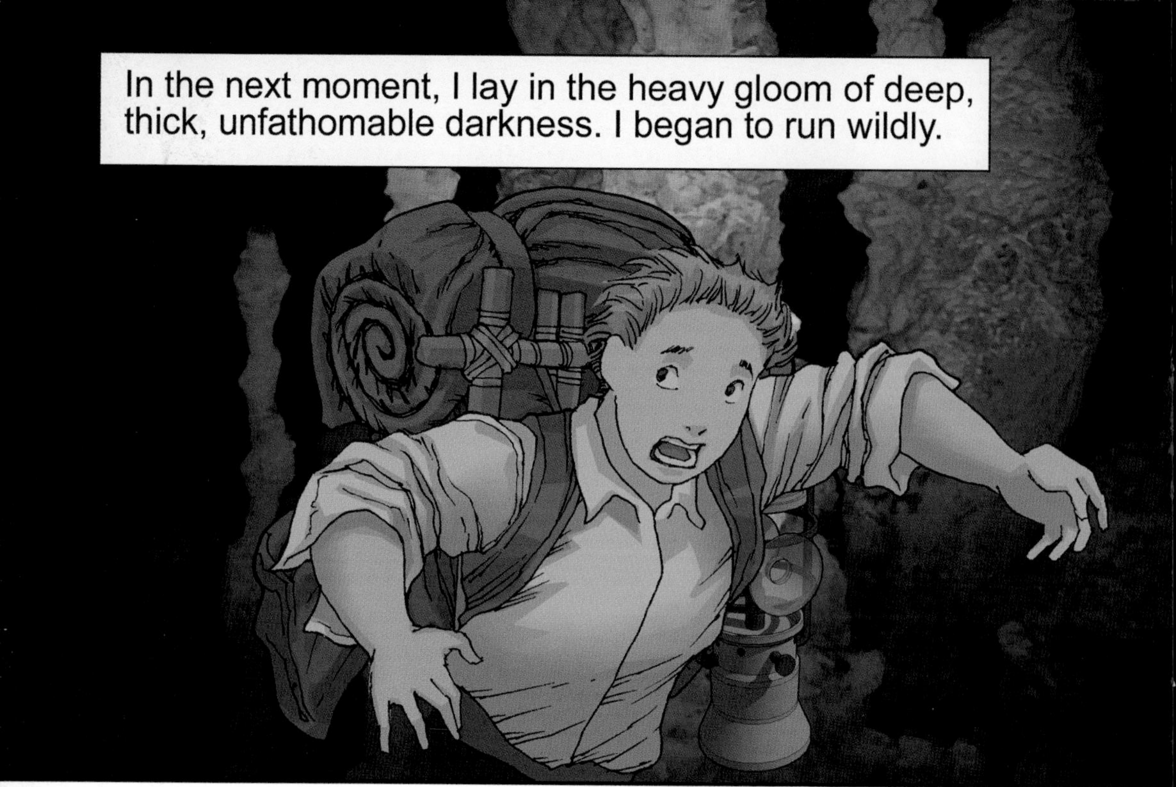
In the next moment, I lay in the heavy gloom of deep, thick, unfathomable darkness. I began to run wildly.

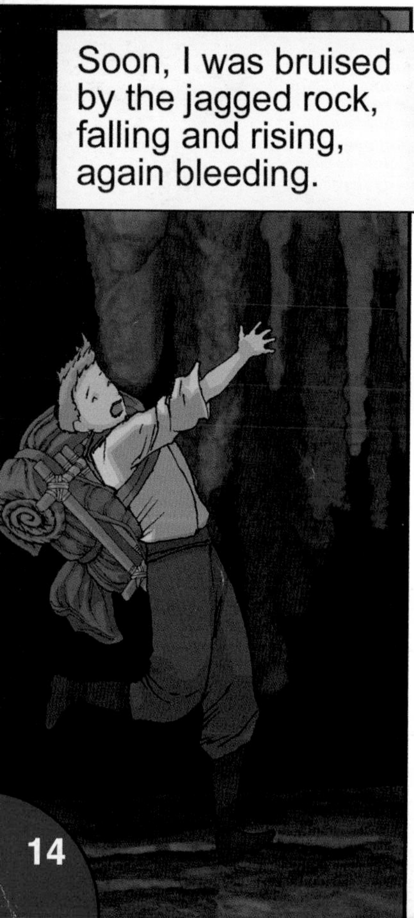
Soon, I was bruised by the jagged rock, falling and rising, again bleeding.

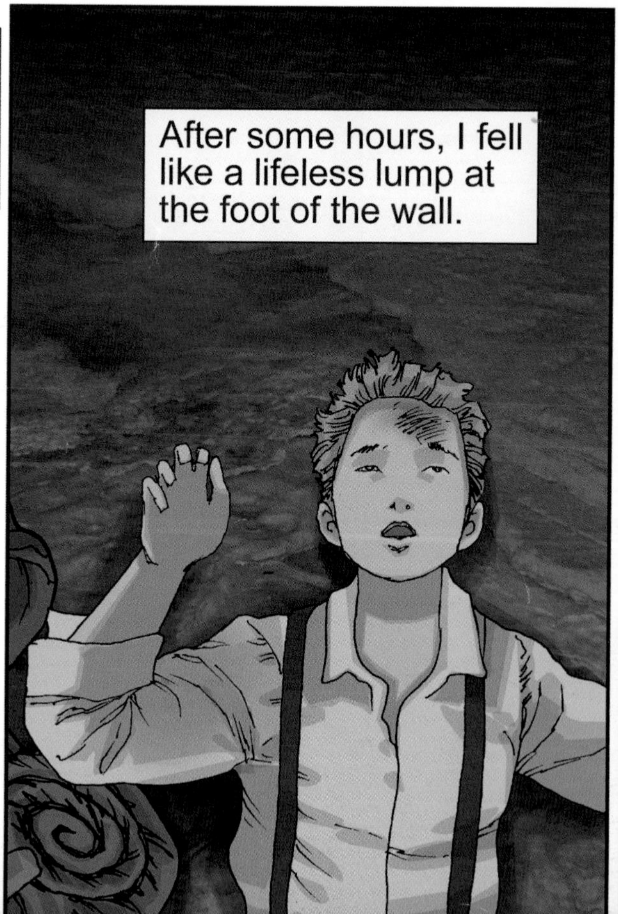
After some hours, I fell like a lifeless lump at the foot of the wall.

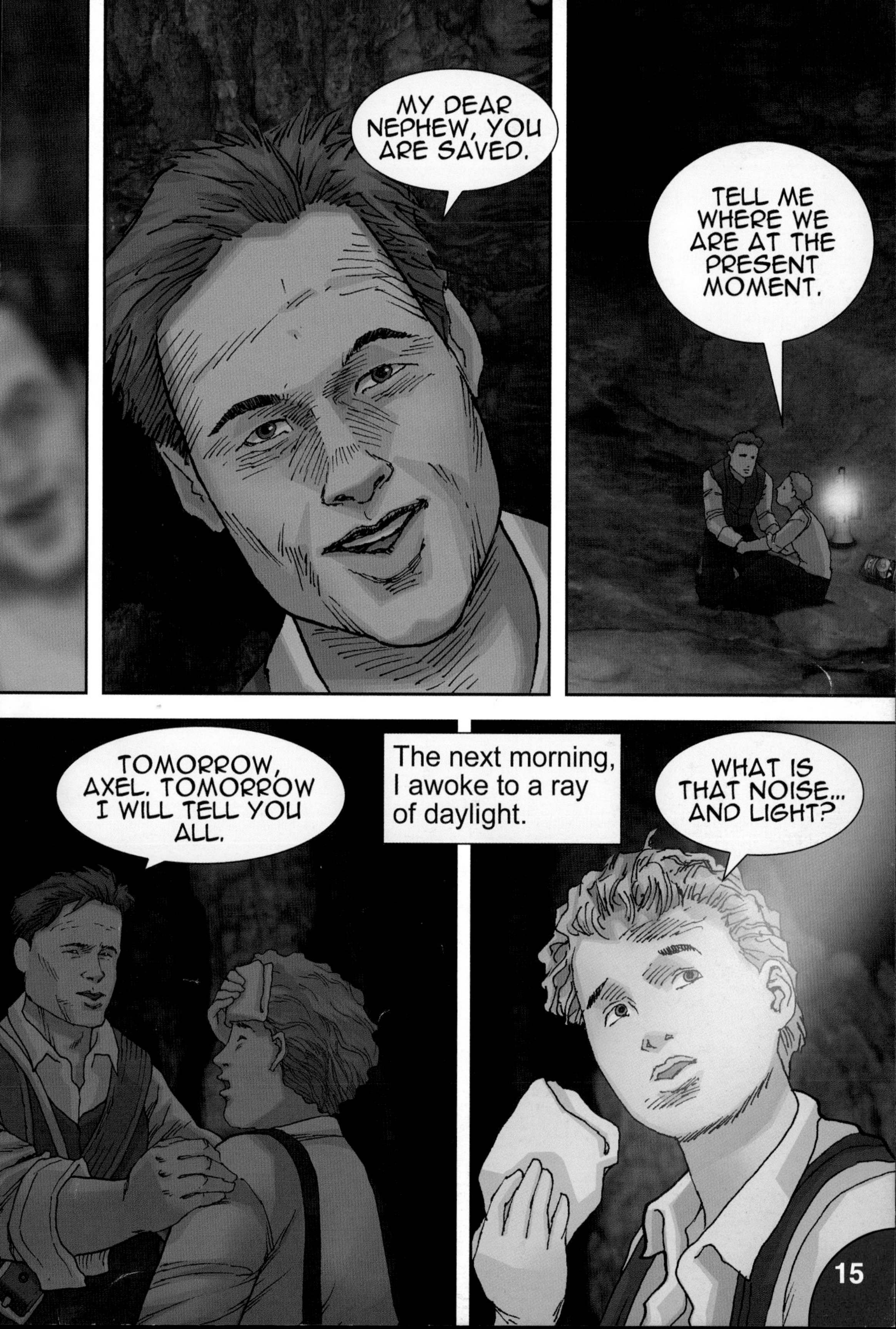
MY DEAR NEPHEW, YOU ARE SAVED.
TELL ME WHERE WE ARE AT THE PRESENT MOMENT.
TOMORROW, AXEL. TOMORROW I WILL TELL YOU ALL.
The next morning, I awoke to a ray of daylight.
WHAT IS THAT NOISE... AND LIGHT?

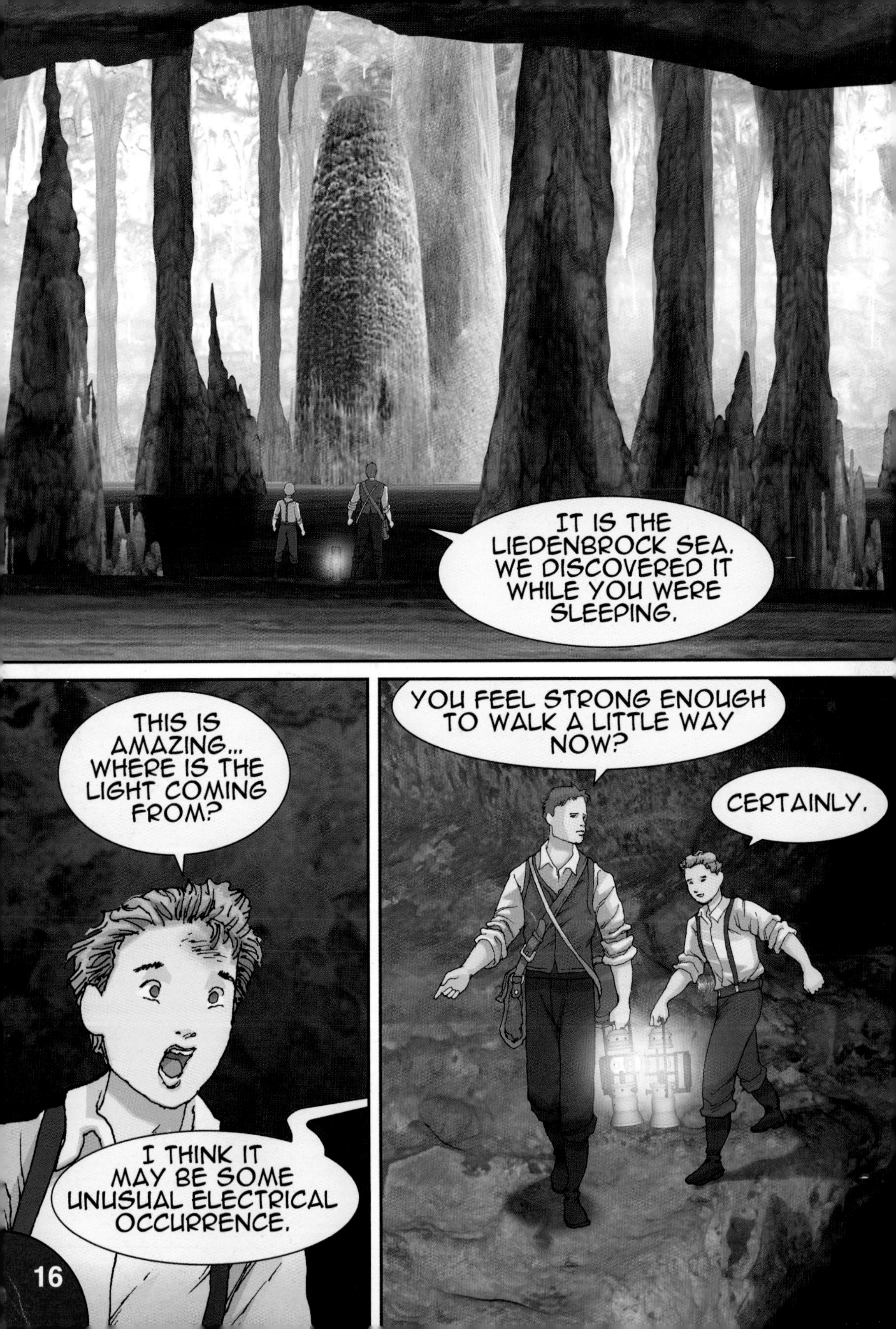
IT IS THE LIEDENBROCK SEA. WE DISCOVERED IT WHILE YOU WERE SLEEPING.
THIS IS AMAZING... WHERE IS THE LIGHT COMING FROM?
I THINK IT MAY BE SOME UNUSUAL ELECTRICAL OCCURRENCE.
YOU FEEL STRONG ENOUGH TO WALK A LITTLE WAY NOW?
CERTAINLY.

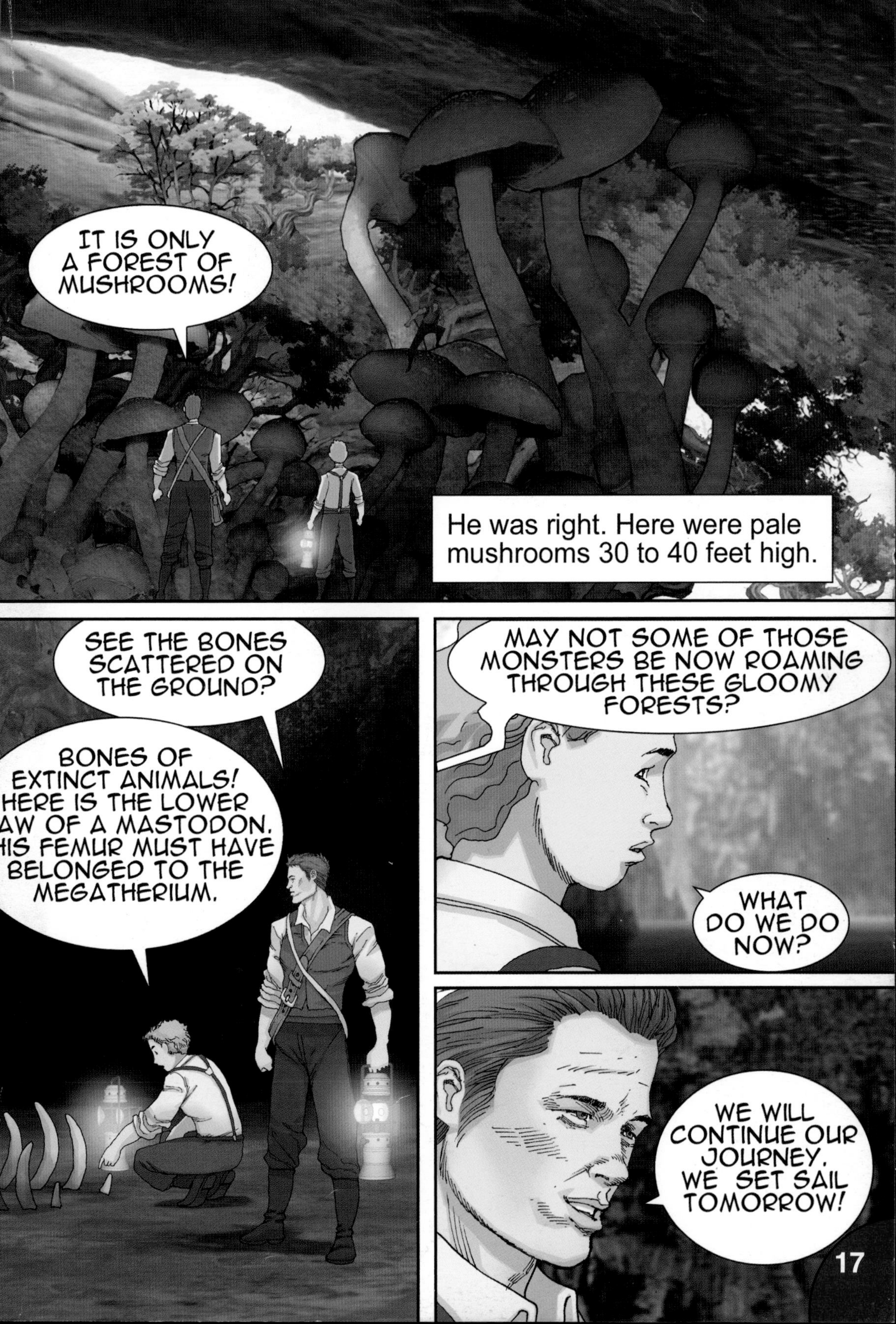

IT IS ONLY A FOREST OF MUSHROOMS!
He was right. Here were pale mushrooms 30 to 40 feet high.
SEE THE BONES SCATTERED ON THE GROUND?
BONES OF EXTINCT ANIMALS! HERE IS THE LOWER JAW OF A MASTODON. THIS FEMUR MUST HAVE BELONGED TO THE MEGATHERIUM.
MAY NOT SOME OF THOSE MONSTERS BE NOW ROAMING THROUGH THESE GLOOMY FORESTS?
WHAT DO WE DO NOW?
WE WILL CONTINUE OUR JOURNEY. WE SET SAIL TOMORROW!

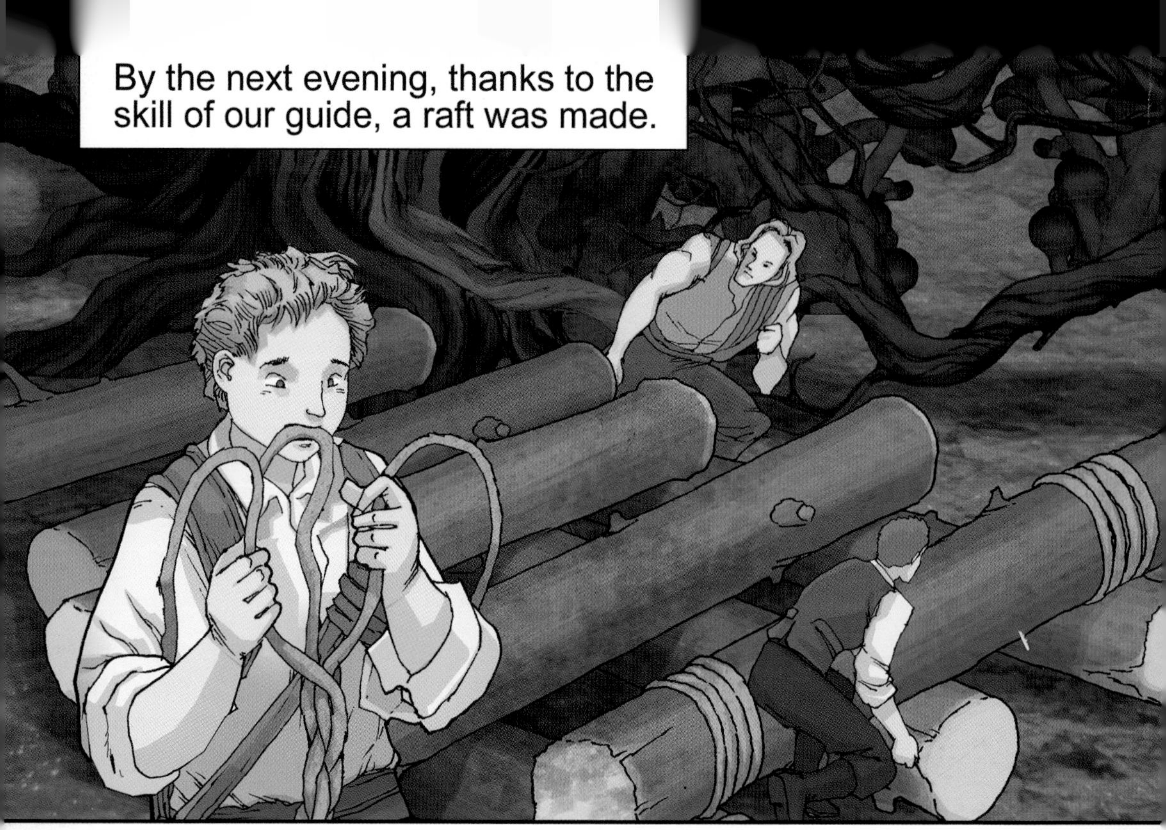
By the next evening, thanks to the skill of our guide, a raft was made.

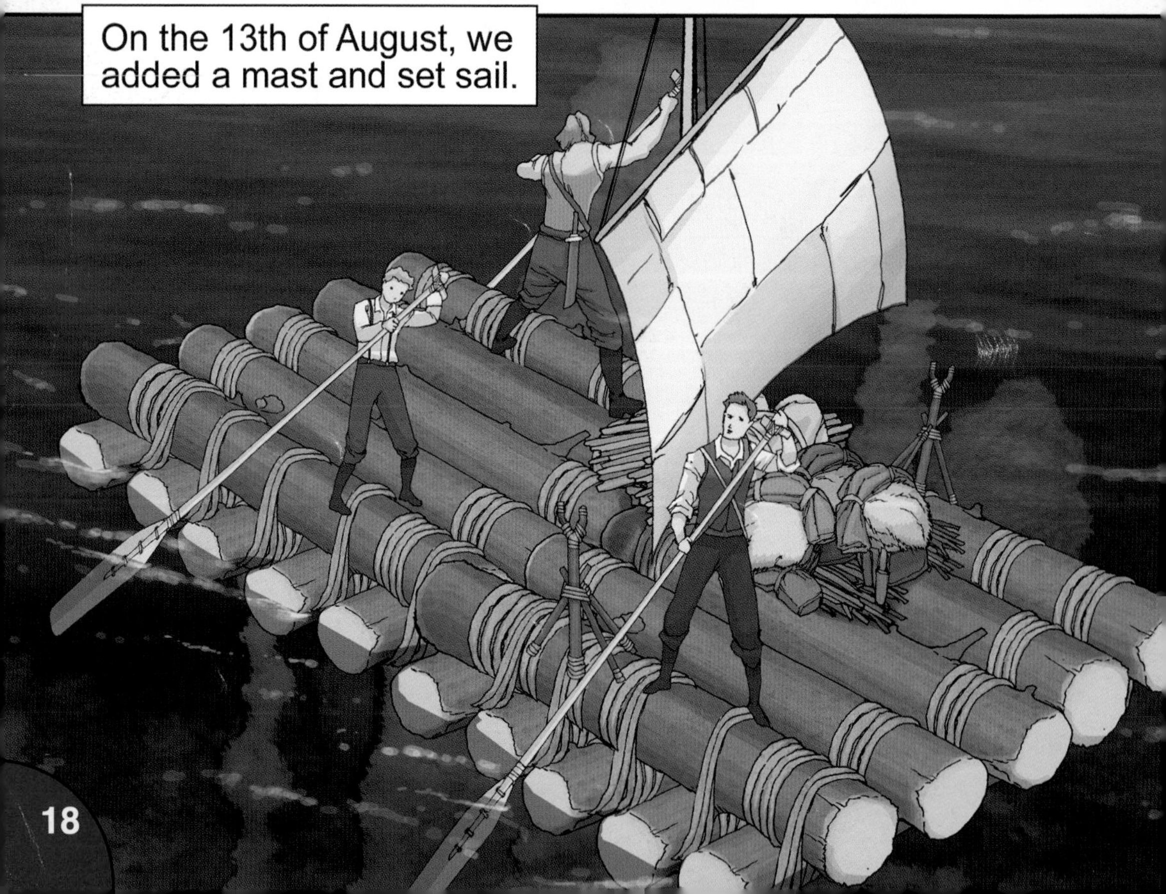
On the 13th of August, we added a mast and set sail.

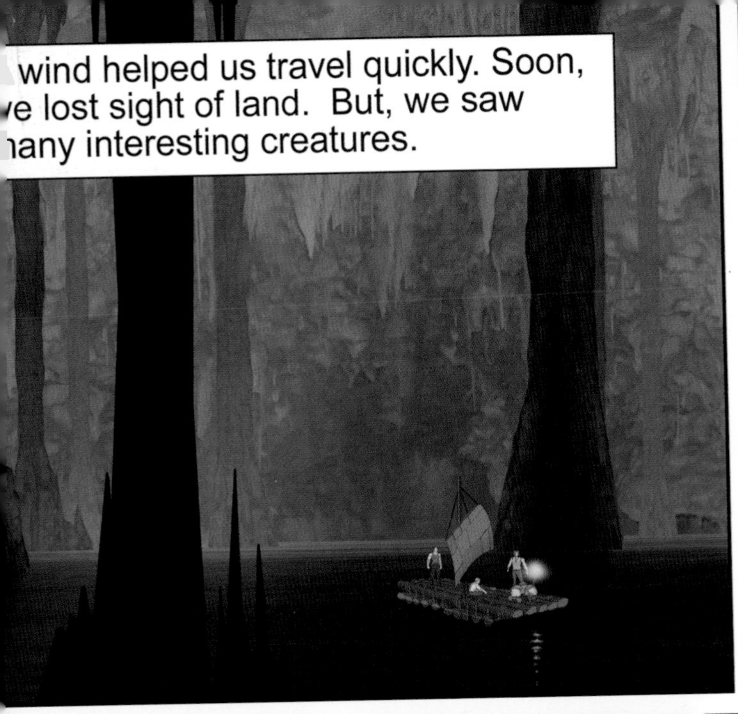
wind helped us travel quickly. Soon,
e lost sight of land. But, we saw
any interesting creatures.

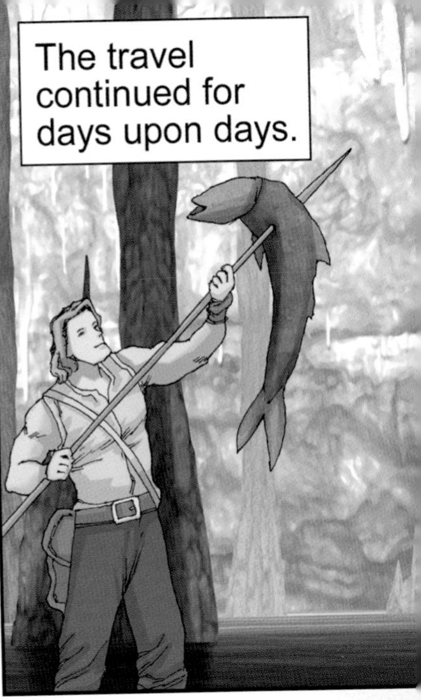
The travel continued for days upon days.

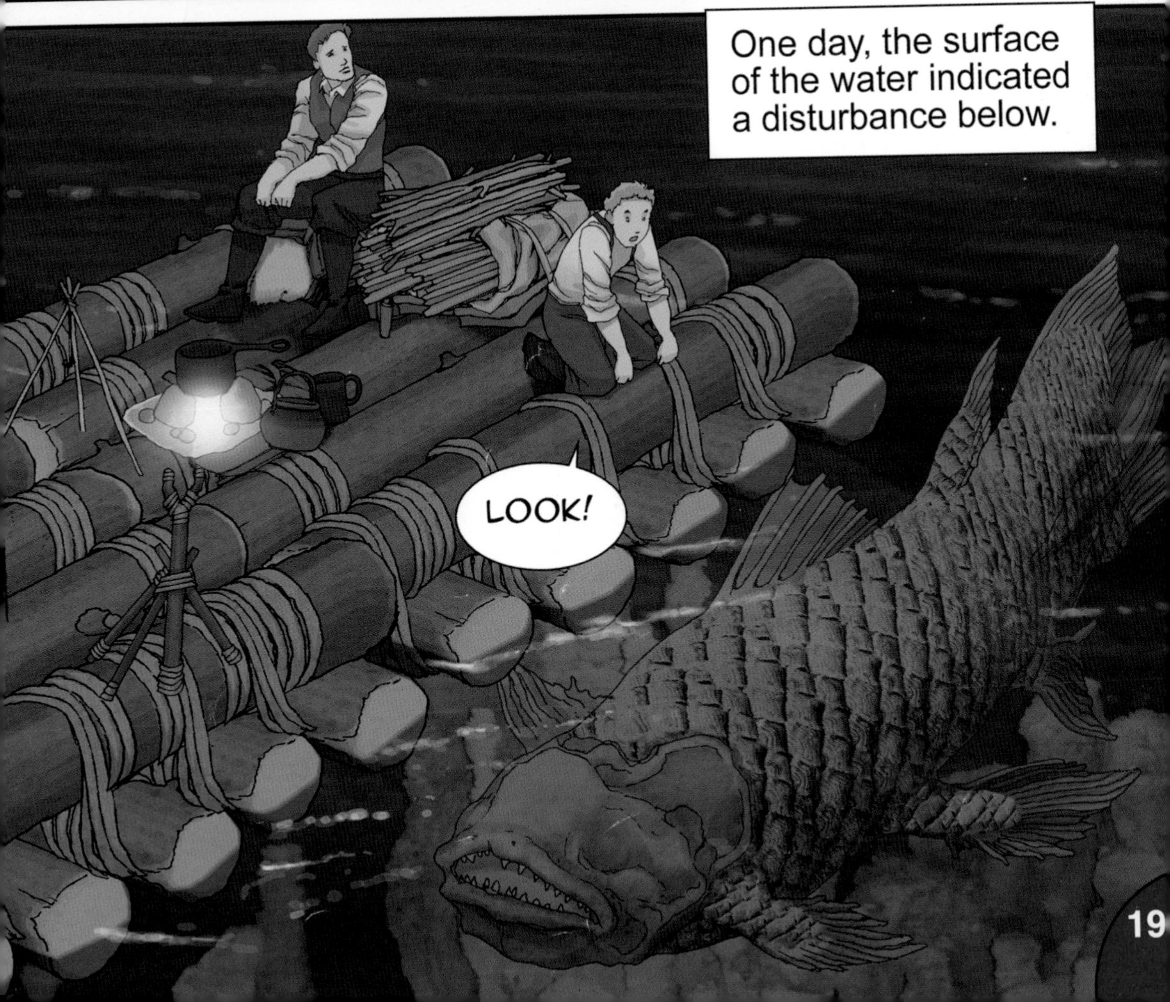
One day, the surface of the water indicated a disturbance below.
LOOK!

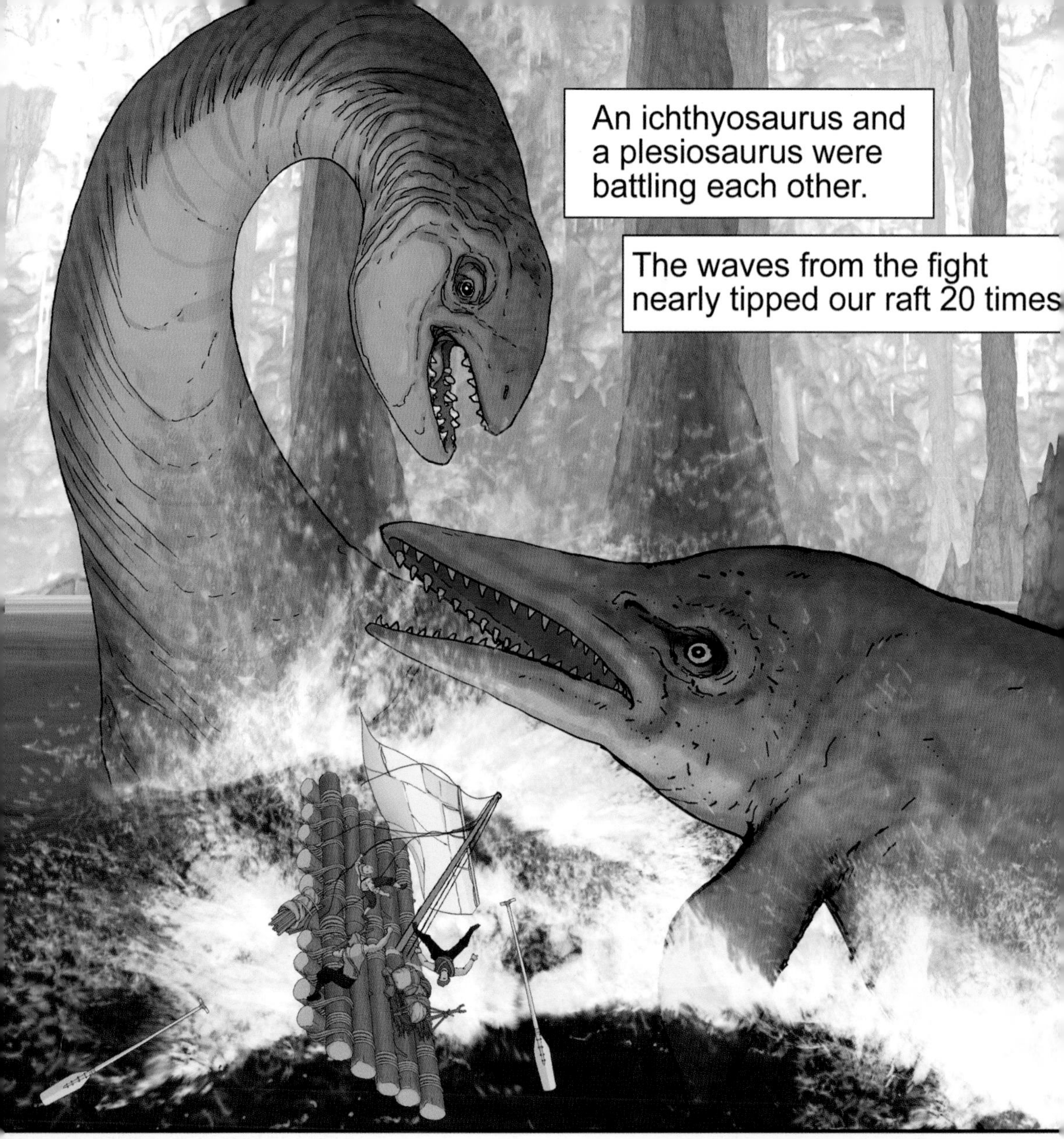
An ichthyosaurus and a plesiosaurus were battling each other.
The waves from the fight nearly tipped our raft 20 times

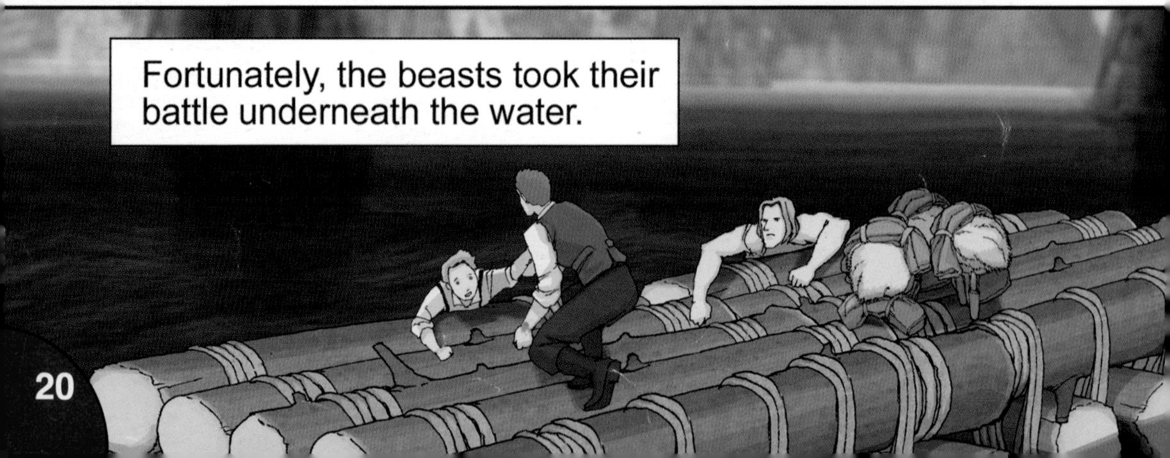
Fortunately, the beasts took their battle underneath the water.

After surviving creatures and storms, we finally arrived onshore.

The next day, the weather was splendid.

My uncle decided we would explore this shore before setting sail again the next day.

LOOK, UNCLE! OVER THERE!

As if we'd traveled back in time, a herd of mastodons appeared.

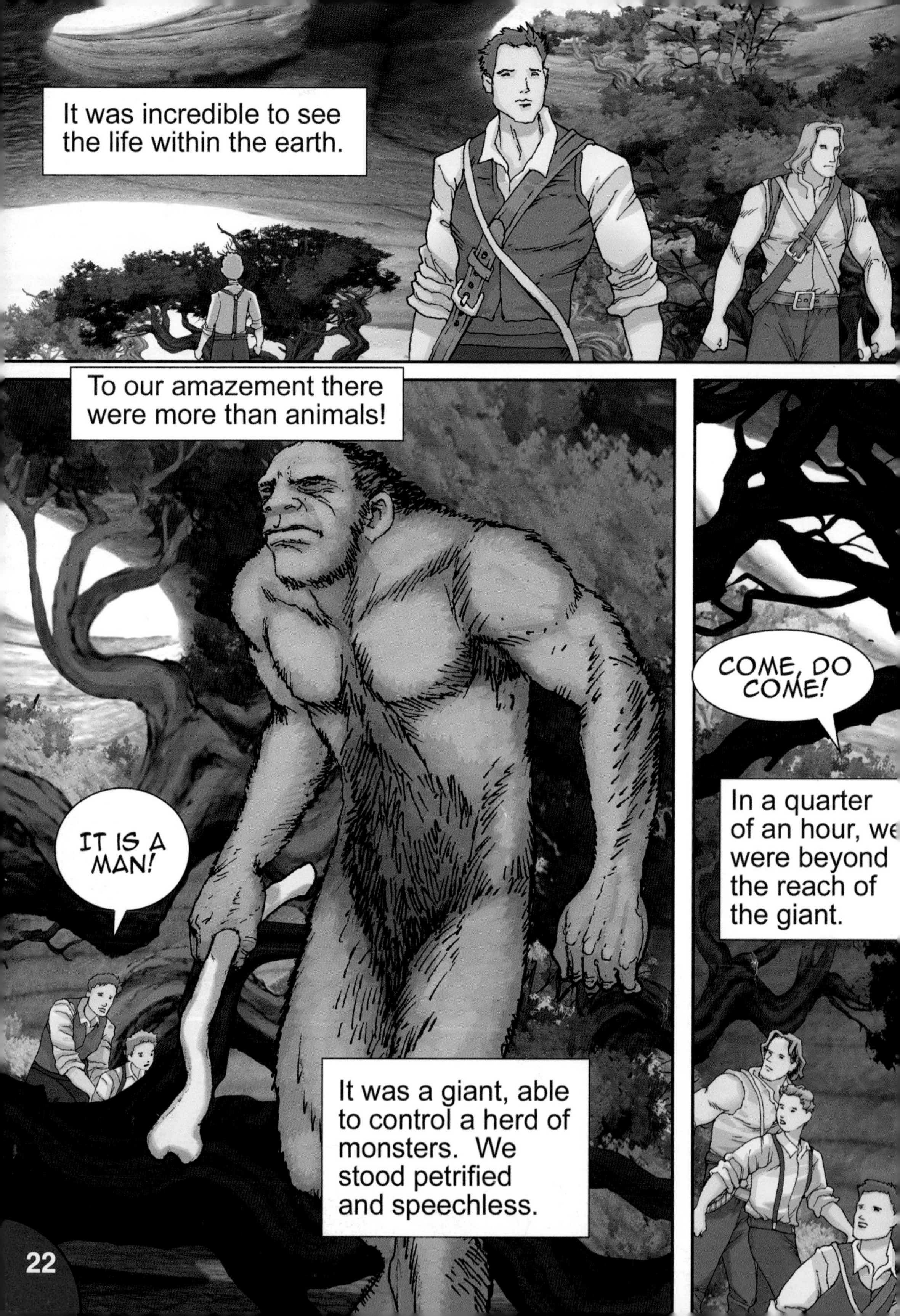
It was incredible to see the life within the earth.
To our amazement there were more than animals!
IT IS A MAN!
It was a giant, able to control a herd of monsters. We stood petrified and speechless.
COME, DO COME!
In a quarter of an hour, we were beyond the reach of the giant.

We decided to look or other tunnels that may lead us farther downward.

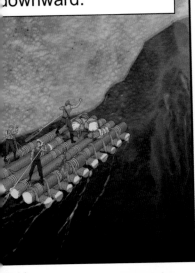

WHY DO WE NOT LOOK OVER THERE?

I THINK I SEE SOME TUNNELS.

HANS, PLEASE HEAD IN THAT DIRECTION.

WELL, LOOK HERE!

LOOK, AS FOR ARNE SAKNUSSEMM. OUR OLD FRIEND HAS BEEN HERE!

THIS TUNNEL APPEARS TO BE BLOCKED BY THIS BOULDER.

IT MUST HAVE FALLEN AFTER SAKNUSSEMM'S PASSAGE.

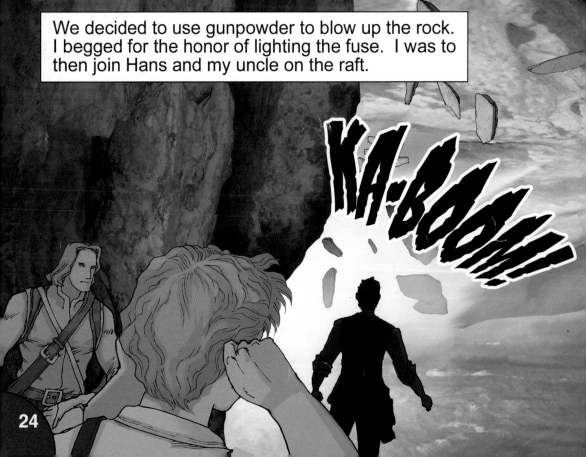

We decided to use gunpowder to blow up the rock. I begged for the honor of lighting the fuse. I was to then join Hans and my uncle on the raft.

KA-BOOM!

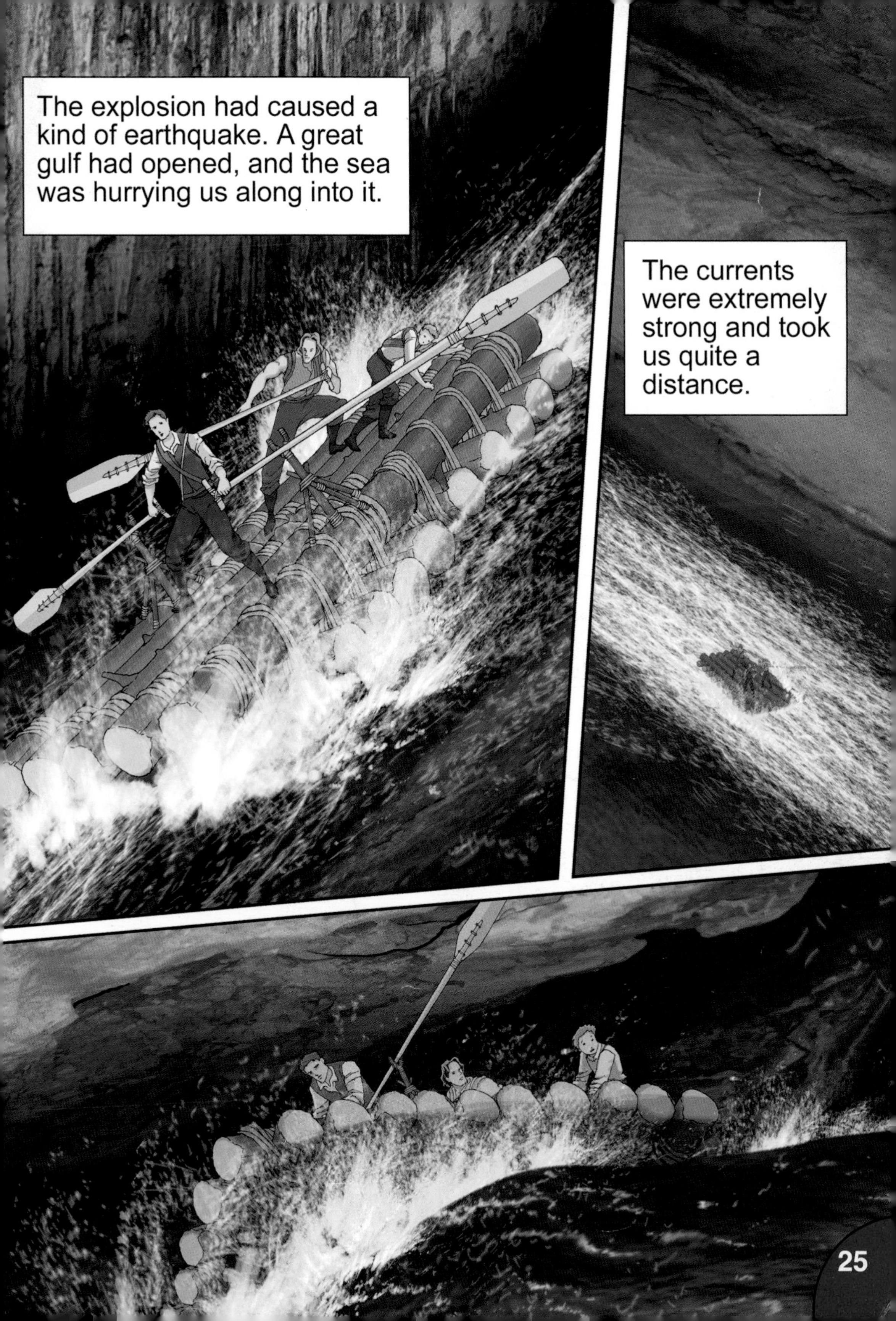
The explosion had caused a kind of earthquake. A great gulf had opened, and the sea was hurrying us along into it.
The currents were extremely strong and took us quite a distance.

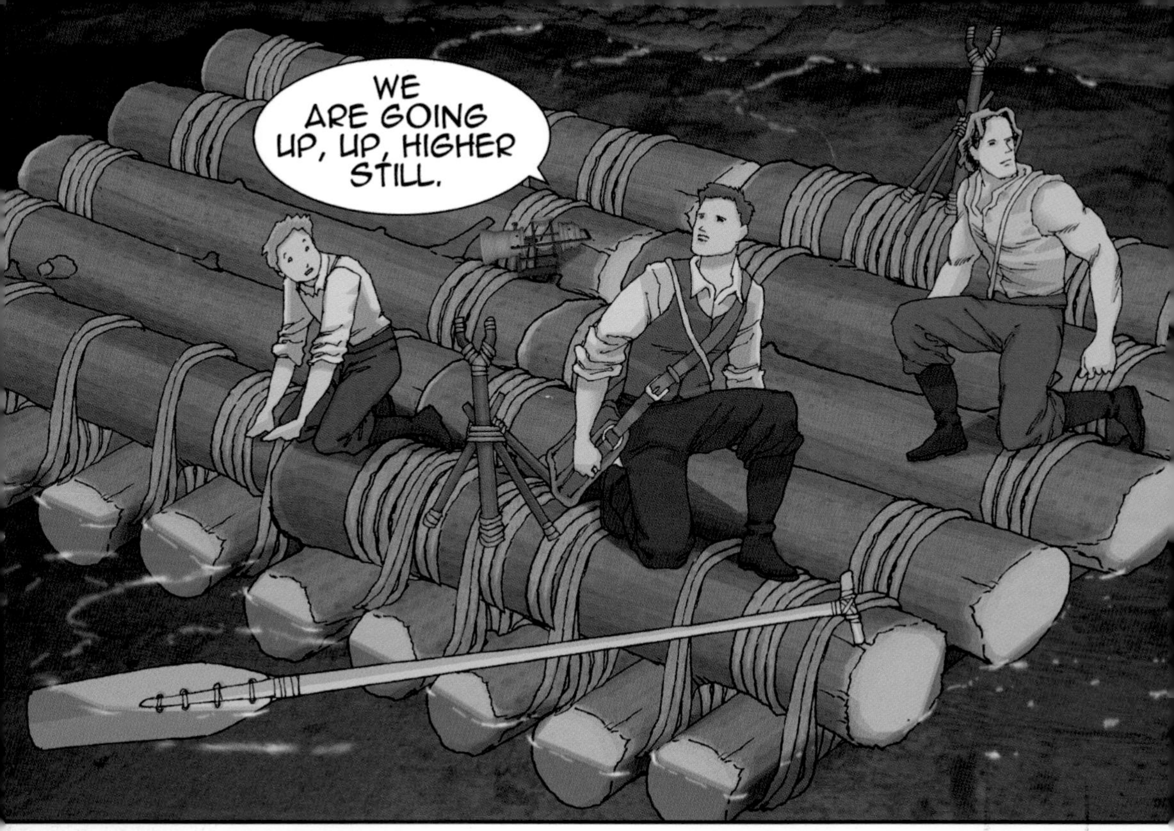
WE ARE GOING UP, UP, HIGHER STILL.

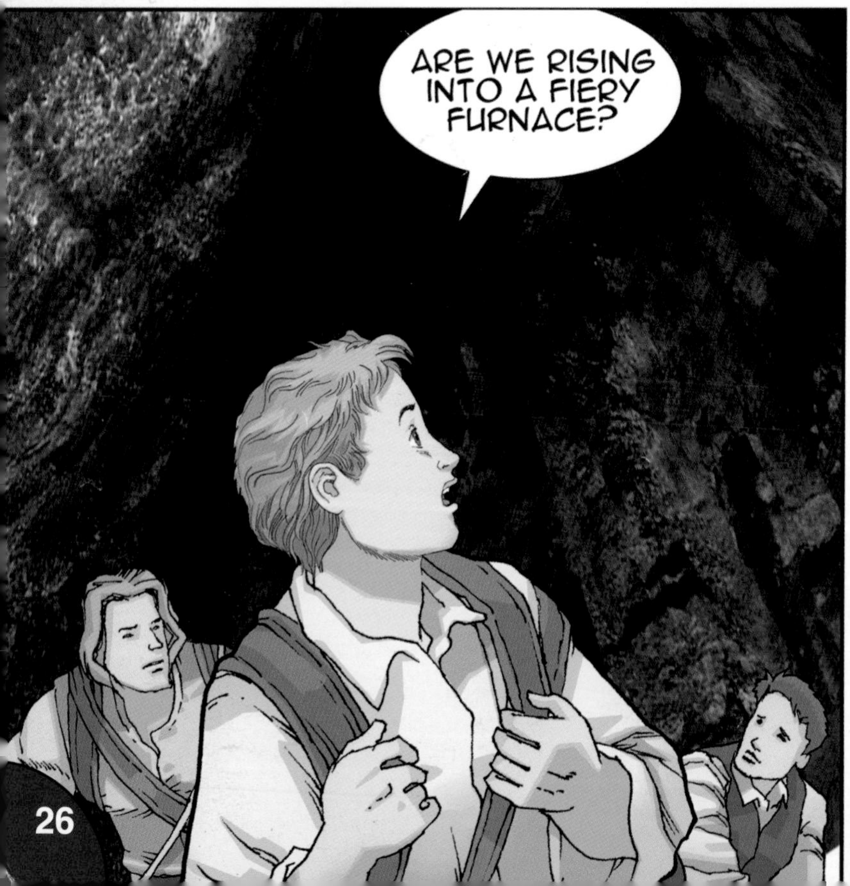
ARE WE RISING INTO A FIERY FURNACE?

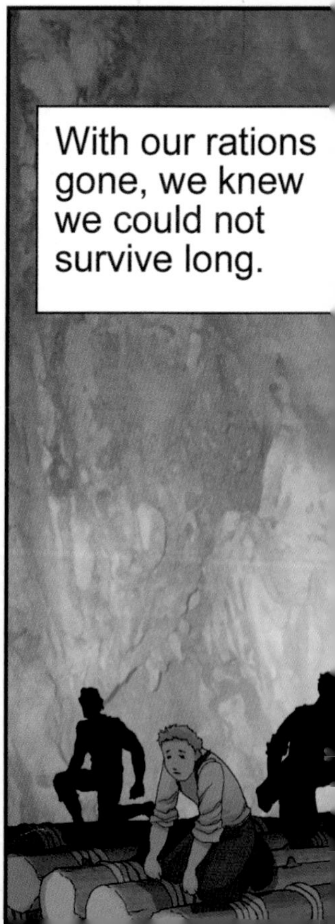
With our rations gone, we knew we could not survive long.

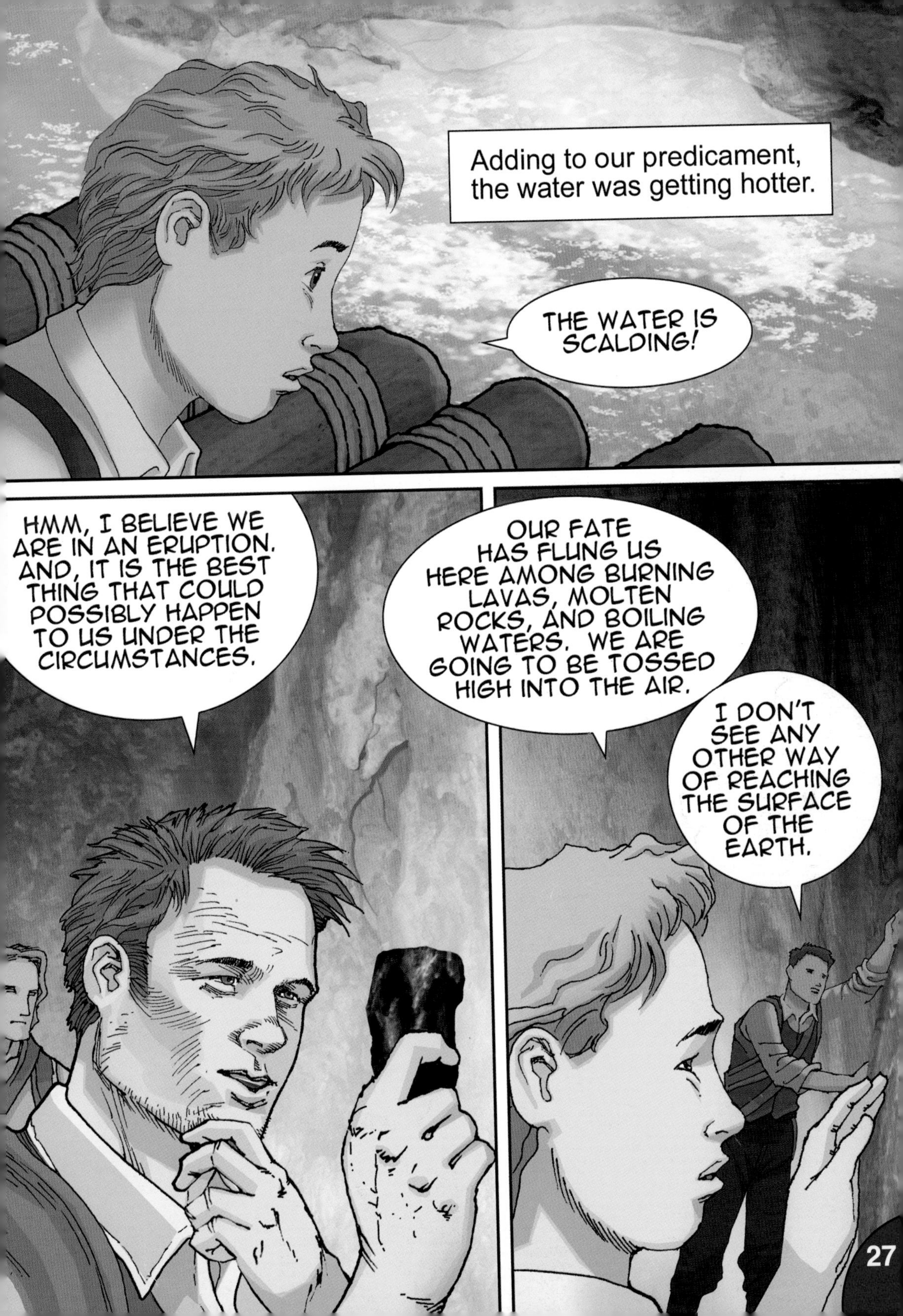
Adding to our predicament, the water was getting hotter.
THE WATER IS SCALDING!
HMM, I BELIEVE WE ARE IN AN ERUPTION. AND, IT IS THE BEST THING THAT COULD POSSIBLY HAPPEN TO US UNDER THE CIRCUMSTANCES.
OUR FATE HAS FLUNG US HERE AMONG BURNING LAVAS, MOLTEN ROCKS, AND BOILING WATERS. WE ARE GOING TO BE TOSSED HIGH INTO THE AIR.
I DON'T SEE ANY OTHER WAY OF REACHING THE SURFACE OF THE EARTH.

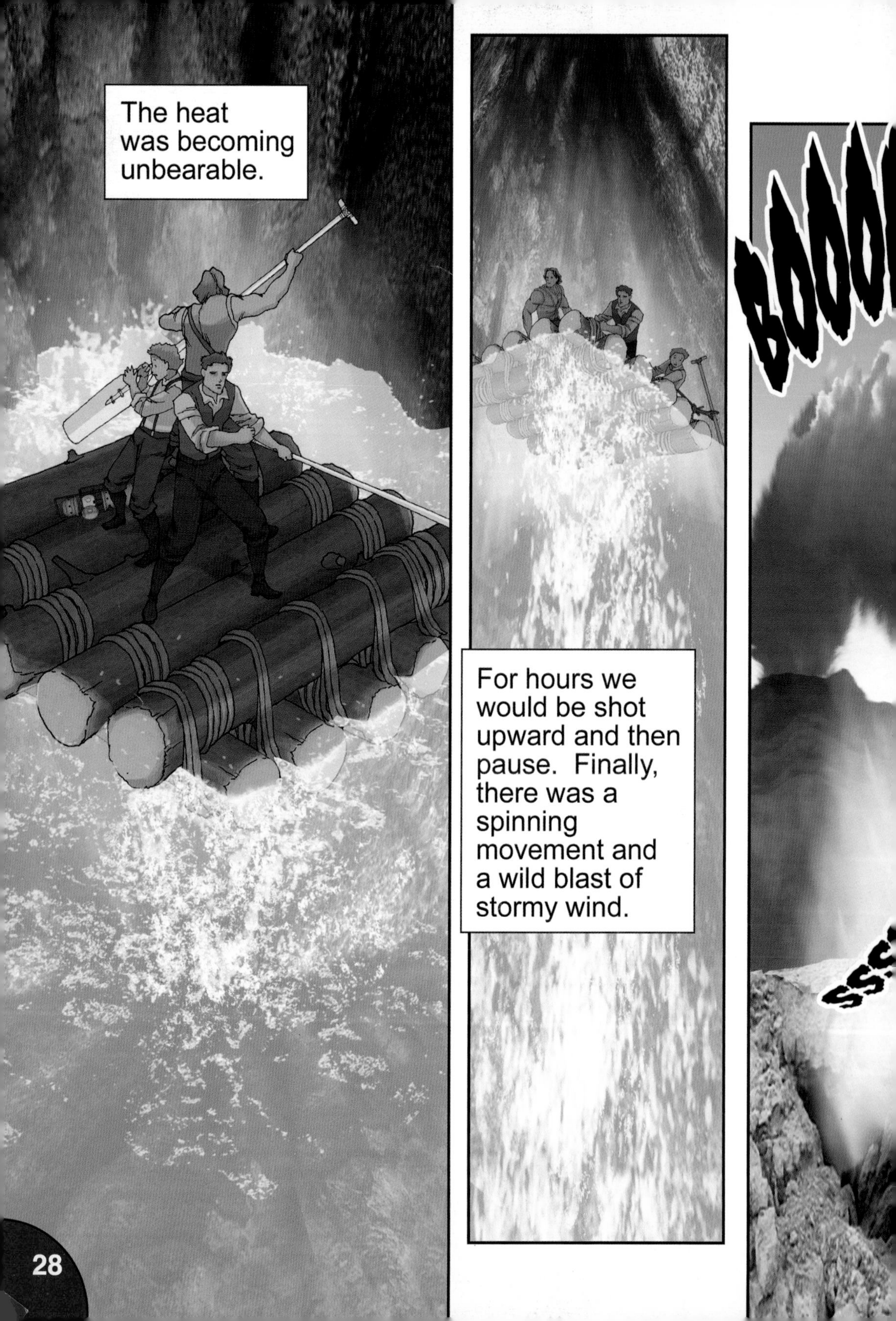
The heat was becoming unbearable.
For hours we would be shot upward and then pause. Finally, there was a spinning movement and a wild blast of stormy wind.

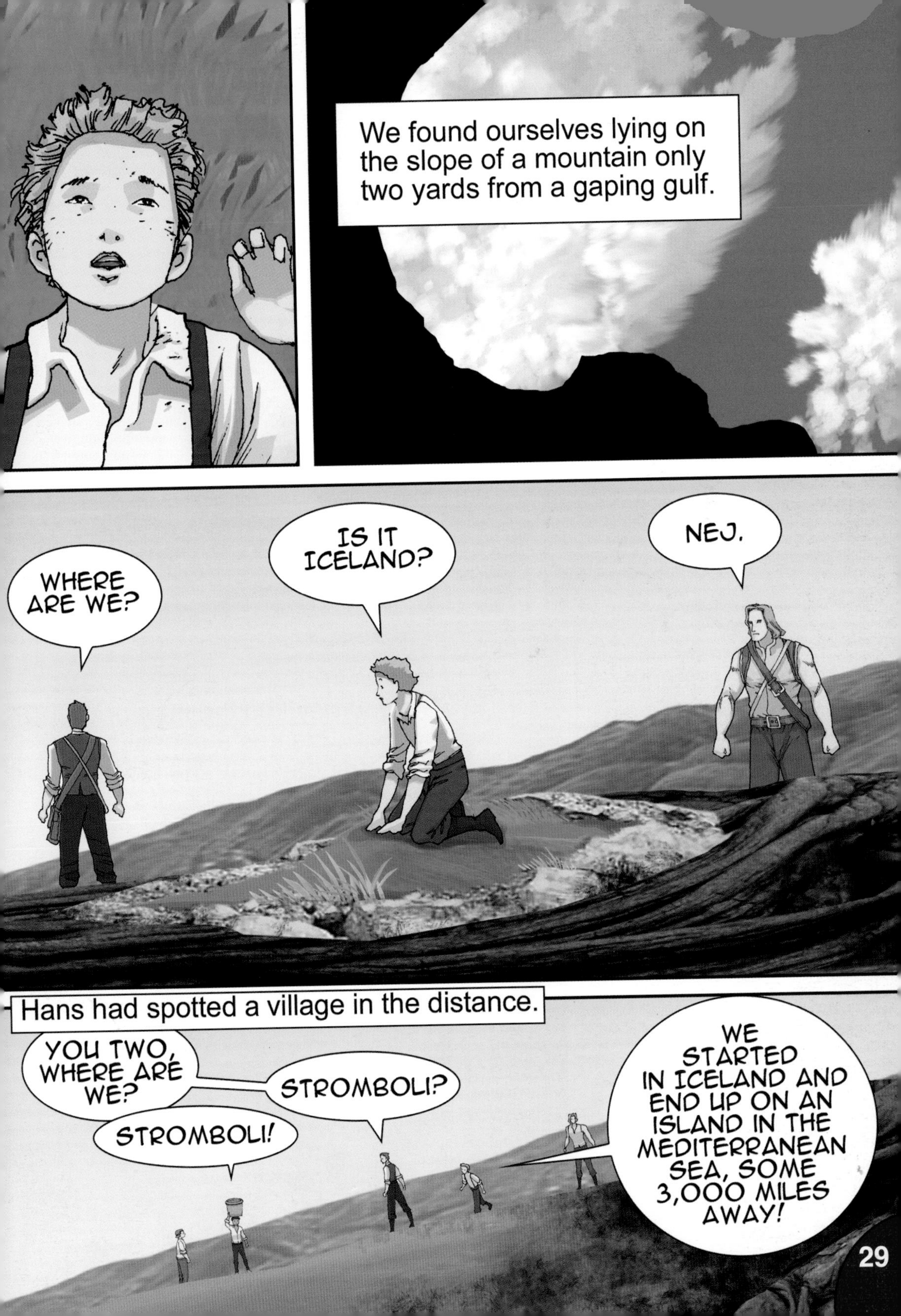
We found ourselves lying on the slope of a mountain only two yards from a gaping gulf.
WHERE ARE WE?
IS IT ICELAND?
NEJ.
Hans had spotted a village in the distance.
YOU TWO, WHERE ARE WE?
STROMBOLI?
STROMBOLI!
WE STARTED IN ICELAND AND END UP ON AN ISLAND IN THE MEDITERRANEAN SEA, SOME 3,000 MILES AWAY!

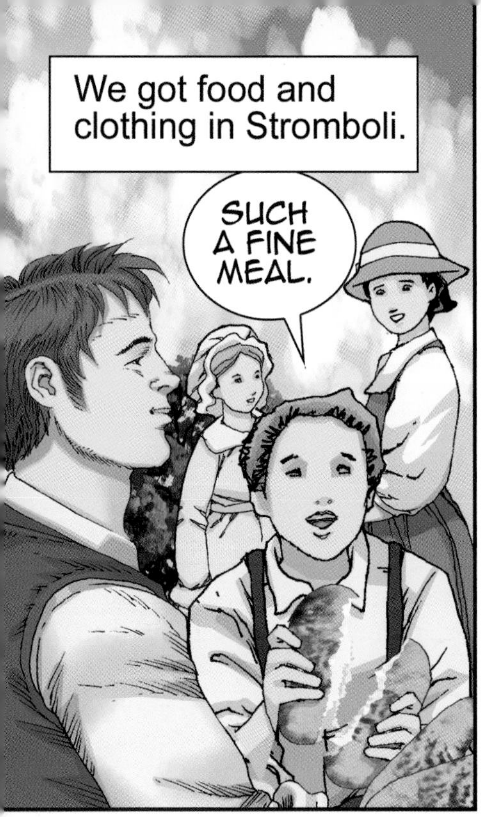
We got food and clothing in Stromboli.
SUCH A FINE MEAL.

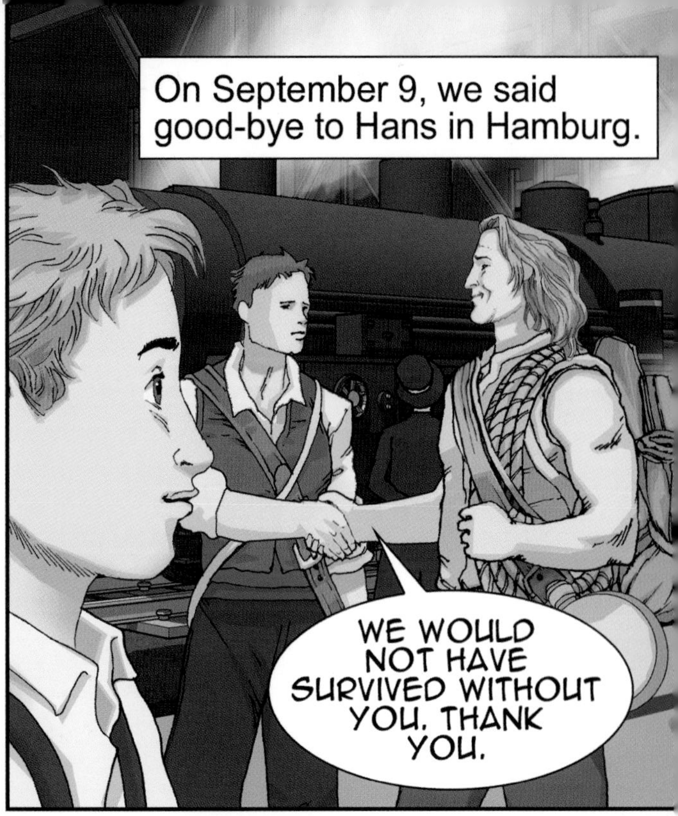
On September 9, we said good-bye to Hans in Hamburg.
WE WOULD NOT HAVE SURVIVED WITHOUT YOU. THANK YOU.

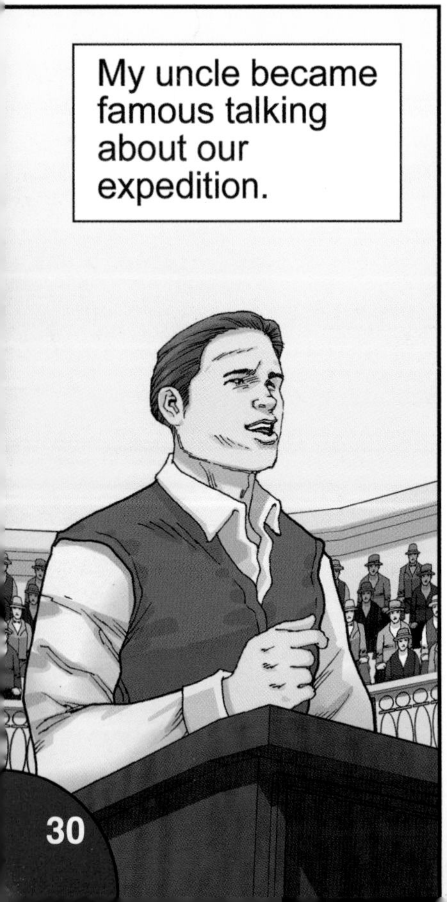
My uncle became famous talking about our expedition.

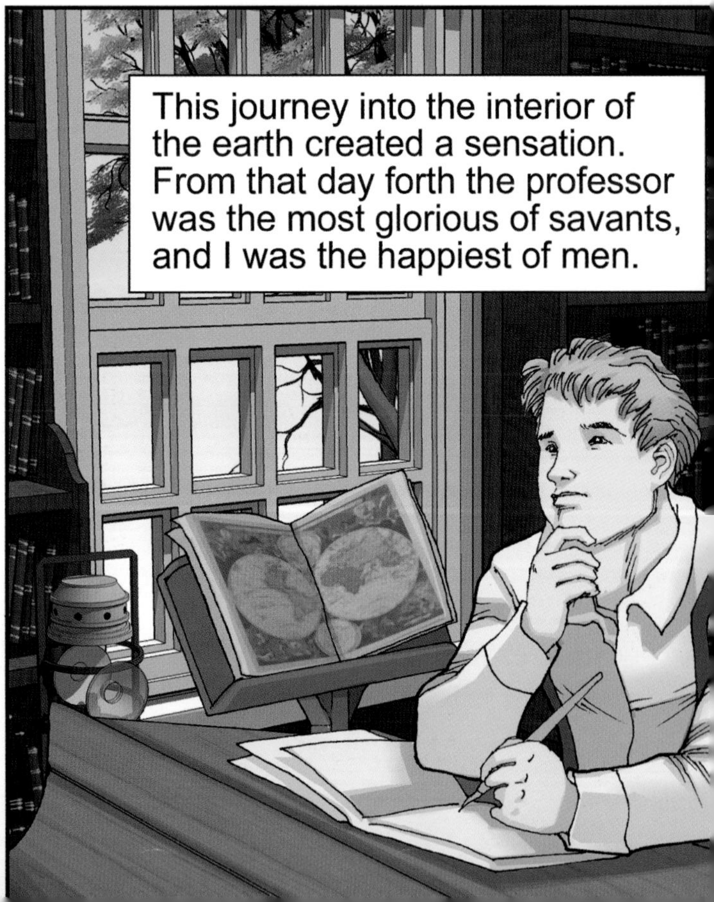
This journey into the interior of the earth created a sensation. From that day forth the professor was the most glorious of savants, and I was the happiest of men.

About the Author

Jules Verne was born on February 8, 1828, in Nantes, France. His father was a lawyer in the port city. Jules always had a love of the sea and tried to run away. His father brought him home and later sent him to Paris to study law. Instead, Jules decided to become a writer.

In 1857, Verne married and became a stockbroker to support his family. He continued to write plays, short stories, and essays. It wasn't until 1863 that Verne quit his job and began writing full-time.

Verne met Jules Hetzel in 1863. Hetzel became Verne's publisher and mentor. He published Verne's first story in his magazine. Verne's work soon became popular. He cleverly included realistic details and explanations that supported his fantastic adventure tales.

Verne died on March 24, 1905, but his son Michel completed and published several of his manuscripts between 1905 and 1919. Today, Jules Verne is often remembered as the father of science fiction. He remains an important influence on many writers.

Additional Works

Five Weeks in a Balloon (1863)
From the Earth to the Moon (1865)
Journey to the Center of the Earth (1867)
Twenty Thousand Leagues Under the Sea (1870)
North Against South (1887)
Floating Island (1895)
The Golden Volcano (1906)
The Chase of the Golden Meteor (1908)

Glossary

alchemist - a person who studies a medieval science of turning something common into something special.

decipher - to interpret or translate by using a key.

descent - movement from a higher place to a lower one.

destination - the place someone or something is going to.

molten - melted by heat.

petrified - to be confused by fear, amazement, or awe.

ration - a fixed amount of food that must last an exact amount of time.

runic - using characters of an alphabet used by German people from 200 to 1200 AD.

savant - a person of learning.

scalding - hot enough to burn someone or something.

Web Sites

To learn more about Jules Verne, visit the ABDO Group online at **www.abdopublishing.com**. Web sites about Verne are featured on our Book Links page. These links are routinely monitored and updated to provide the most current information available.